RESISTANCE KINGS FACE

Apostle Prof. Johnson Suleman

RESISTANCE KINGS FACE

Apostle Prof. Johnson Suleman
Copyright@2024

Published in Nigeria by
Hosanna Publishers
Km 132 Benin-Okene/ Abuja Express way,
Auchi, Edo State, Nigeria
Tel: +2348106468478

CONTENTS

INTRODUCTION

Progression in life is as important as the process. Opposition is evidence of progress. No one faces any resistance except they make what while moves. Eliab saw the threat David posed in ascending to headship. It is a contest that leads to conquests. If you face no challenge, you can't emerge the champion. Trophies are not handed over to winners until at the end of the tournament. The rigour of the competition is the minimum price the winner must pay for the prize. No one will celebrate you until you endure to the end. Only an athlete who touches the finishing line is adjudged the winner. To finish is not enough, you must finish well and properly. You must understand that the world is too busy to notice Mr. Nobodies. Except you present a pre-qualification testimony, the king may never endorse you.

Don't be in a hurry to present you before the king. Stay behind the doors and focus on preparation. Only those who are prepared see opportunity when they are thrown around. What people lament over as problems is what takes a few to limelight. The unprepared Israelites troop saw Goliath as a challenge, but David climbed on it as a ladder. How do you see troubles? They will always occur in life but see them as amplifiers. If you are ill-prepared the challenge magnifies your weakness. To those who are properly equipped, it is a mere ceremonial coronation of a king. No matter how much God loves you, He will never give you a trophy without a trial. Temptations and trials are the road map to the top of life and destiny. Even Christ Jesus faced the fury of Herod before the endorsement at river Jordan. "This is my beloved son…" is only for victors. You can't be a son until you have been tested and tried.

The entire universe is waiting for your manifestation. You must scale all the hurdles to be celebrated. It is possible. Nevertheless, there are potholes you must avoid. If Joseph hadn't fled the forceful grip of Potiphar's wife, his destiny would have been amputated. You must be sensitive to the traps of the devil. He monitors champions carefully with the intention to limit them. Don't sell your destiny for a morsel of bread. You can't be smart enough to overcome the serpent. He has been around for a long time. It takes intimacy with God to enjoy victory. The closer you go to God, the easier it becomes to resist the devil. So, the first rule of resistance is due submission to the Master. His words are your guiding light. You can't fall if you learn to stay in the word. Don't expect a bright future if fellowship with the word is not optimized. How much you know Him is the much the world knows you.

Read this; embrace greatness.

THE FOUNDATION OF ROYALTY

THE FOUNDATION OF ROYALTY

he LORD *do so and much more to Jonathan: but if it please my father to do thee evil, then I will shew it thee, and send thee away, that thou mayest go in peace: and the* LORD *be with thee, as he hath been with my father. So David hid himself in the field: and when the new moon was come, the king sat him down to eat meat. And the king sat upon his seat, as at other times, even upon a seat by the wall: and Jonathan arose, and Abner sat by Saul's side, and David's place was empty. Nevertheless Saul spake not any thing that day: for he thought, Something hath befallen him, he is not clean; surely he is not clean. And it came to pass on the morrow, which was the second day of the month, that David's place was empty: and Saul said unto Jonathan his son, Wherefore cometh not the son of Jesse to meat, neither yesterday, nor to day? And Jonathan answered Saul, David earnestly asked leave of me to go to Bethlehem: And he said, Let me go, I pray thee; for our family hath a sacrifice in the city; and my brother, he hath commanded me to be there: and now, if I have found favour in thine eyes, let me get away, I pray thee, and see my brethren. Therefore he cometh not unto the king's table. Then Saul's anger was kindled against Jonathan, and he said unto him, Thou son of the perverse rebellious woman, do not I know that thou hast chosen the son of Jesse to thine own confusion, and unto the confusion of thy mother's nakedness? For as long as the son of Jesse liveth upon the ground, thou shalt not be established, nor thy kingdom. Wherefore now send and fetch him unto me, for he shall surely die. And*

It was Martin Luther King Jr who said, *"You don't have to see the whole staircase, just take the first step."* Every challenge comes with fear. The effrontery to stand up against intimidation is the victory dance. You can't reign except you fight. If you don't encounter opposition, it is because there is no empty throne before you. No one will come after you as long as you remain in your father's house. In the anchor test, I Samuel 20:13, 24-33, David became a target of attack instead of being celebrated. No one bothered David as long as Goliath lived. The killing of Goliath was the first step to the throne. Saul knew it. The women sang it because it was an open secret. Saul understood the implication

The effrontery to stand up against intimidation is the victory dance.

of abandoning the fight between the Philistines and Israel (I Samuel 20:31). The establishment of Saul or Jonathan's throne became dependent on the absence of David. People don't succeed suddenly; it is a careful and thoughtful plan that leads to the enthronement of kings.

There is no bright future anywhere; it is the illumination of the day that brightens tomorrow.

I have even heard of thee, that the spirit of the gods is in thee, and that light and understanding and excellent wisdom is found in thee. {Daniel 5:14 KJV}

Expectedly, the triumph of David over Goliath would have enlisted celebration within the inner cycle of Saul. The reverse was rather the case. Your adversaries understand that your ability to scale the hurdle means access to the throne. For every obstacle you overcome, there is a throne place before you. There must always be a contest before acquisition. Victories are in-born. Until you possess the light, you can't light up your future. Get the light now, so the future will be bright. The past can't be altered. What you do now presents a better tomorrow. David went through personal practice and rigour for the ultimate contest. Except you prepare, opportunity means nothing. Success is the timely combination of preparation and opportunity.

I returned, and saw under the sun, that the race is not to the swift, nor the battle to the strong, neither yet bread to the wise, nor yet riches to men of understanding, nor yet favour to men of skill; but time and chance happeneth to them all. {Ecc. 9:11 KJV}

Challenges are steps that take the ordinary man into royalty. You can't go back and change the beginning. However, you can do something today that changes the beginning. If you were born into a poor family, for instance, you can't unborn yourself; but you can change the tide. Perhaps, only few people knew Jesse in Israel until David defeated Goliath. Instead of

Challenges are steps that take the ordinary man into royalty.

David bemoaning his birthplace, he positioned himself for greatness. Results are the fastest bells that announce a man in obscurity. He reversed the effect of the past. The background could not keep his back on the ground.

And Eliab his eldest brother heard when he spake unto the men; and Eliab's anger was kindled against David, and he said, Why camest thou down hither? and with whom hast thou left those few sheep in the wilderness? I know thy pride, and the naughtiness of thine heart; for thou art come down that thou mightest see the battle. And David said, What have I now done? Is there not a cause? {**I Samuel 17:28-29 KJV**}

At about 16 years of age, the siblings of David already discriminated against him. David was not allowed to be present at the August visit of Samuel to the family. He was sent to the field for the grazing of the livestock. No doubt, the star of

Ascension to greatness is never a funfair.

kingship on him attracted his being sidelined. You will always be resisted if you are destined for the throne. Ascension to greatness is never a funfair. The forces on the earth will oppose you. David was manipulated to the bush for herding when he should have been the chief host of Samuel. It took the prophetic maturity of Samuel to detect that David was left out.

Again, Jesse made seven of his sons to pass before Samuel. And Samuel said unto Jesse, The LORD hath not chosen these. And Samuel said unto Jesse, Are here all thy children? And he said, There remaineth yet the youngest, and, behold, he keepeth the sheep. And Samuel said unto Jesse, Send and fetch him: for we will not sit down till he come hither. And he sent, and brought him in. Now he was ruddy, and withal of a beautiful countenance, and goodly to look to. And the LORD said, Arise, anoint him: for this is he.
{I Samuel 16:10-12 KJV}

It is dangerous to be oblivious of the contention over every prophecy on your head. About the age of 9 years, God spoke to Samuel in Eli's temple.

And the L*ORD* *came, and stood, and called as at other times, Samuel, Samuel. Then Samuel answered, Speak; for thy servant heareth. And the* L*ORD* *said to Samuel, Behold, I will do a thing in Israel, at which both the ears of every one that heareth it shall tingle. In that day I will perform against Eli all things which I have spoken concerning his house: when I begin, I will also make an end.* **{1 Samuel 3:10-12 KJV}**

If you carefully analyse the incident, David became the eventual beneficiary years later. How? The retirement of Eli initiated the process of God's direct rulership over Israel. Samuel was a forerunner to anoint and guide the first king of Israel. Saul was not the pioneer king. He was a necessary process to the enthronement of the king. I Samuel 9:16, God sent Samuel to anoint Saul a captain over Israel. The mix-up between Eli and to the eventual ascension to the throne by Saul was a direct contention over David's kingship. Saul was designed to usher in David. He was sent as the chief of army staff to enthrone the king. Unfortunately, he overstayed his welcome.

John the Baptist was Saul's type of the New Testament dispensation. John the Baptist's ministry ended as soon as Christ Jesus came to the scene. Nevertheless, he stayed put. The exhaustion of his message became evident in the incursion into Herodia's marital affairs. John the Baptist had no mandate to amend marriages. His preoccupation was the announcement of the King of kings in human flesh.

And said unto him, Art thou he that should come, or do we look for another {**Matthew 11:3 KJV**}

The prince of this world intended to use John the Baptist to cast controversy on Christ's assignment. In Matthew 11:1-9, John the Baptist's emissary and question were unnecessary. It was a contest of

Christ's Kingship. Otherwise, how do you juxtapose his earlier declaration, "*… behold, the Lamb of God that takes away the sins of the world…*" with the later confusion. Your mandate is effectively deflected if the man who announced it later expressed doubt. Except doubt is eliminated mission can't be fulfilled. The focal point was the kingdom of Christ on earth. No king emerges without strong resistance. If Christ Jesus faced this on earth, you will. Don't cry over the incessant gang up against you. Kings don't find it easy before they

are coroneted. Again, the death of Saul was not an automatic ascension to the throne by David. In II Samuel 2, Abner fought David as soon as the father left the scene ingloriously.

And there was a very sore battle that day; and Abner was beaten, and the men of Israel, before the servants of David. {II Samuel 2:17 KJV}

Therefore, Saul was not the problem. Saul was only a tool to stop David's decoration over Israel. Several times we erroneously focus on individuals, instead of the assignment. More often than not, it is the future ahead of you that initiates the battle. The devil won't fight you if he has not seen the crown ahead. He sees your reign in the land, he projects ahead to stop your possessing the land. The antidote, therefore, is advance into the land.

PROCESS PREPARES KINGS

PROCESS PREPARES KINGS

Therefore thus saith the Lord G*od*, Behold, I lay in Zion for a foundation a stone, a tried stone, a precious corner stone, a sure foundation: he that believeth shall not make haste.* {Isaiah 28:16 KJV}

Could God not just have brought David around as the first king of Israel? Why must Samuel pass through the tutelage of Eli? Did David really need the blessings and the endorsement of Saul before confronting Goliath? There are myriads of questions that may never find a point-blank answer as far as human endeavours are concerned. The time lag between every prophecy and its fulfillment is a process. Process comes in different shapes and colours. The necessity of process can only be appreciated at the top. There is no history without a story. God's lifting is through steps. Principles are the staircase of life. No one will care about ethics and principles if not for the inevitable hindrance. Accessing prominence takes patience and endurance. We talk often about faith but forget patience. Nobody will learn any lesson except the one process imposes. Improvement comes on the bedrock of process. Though David was not yet in the picture, but God already foretold Samuel about David. Every spoken word of God will come to fusion at its due time. What God told Samuel at the age of 9 years, came to pass when he was 75 years old. Lessons are pillars that keep the future together. In an architectural edifice, without the pillars, the foundation can't hold the roofing.

Therefore whosoever heareth these sayings of mine, and doeth them, I will liken him unto a wise man, which built his house upon a rock: {**Matthew 7:24 KJV**}

So many people are impatient to allow prophecy work out itself. You can't help God to answer your prayer. While you must do the needful, you must learn to rest. Prophecies are prayer points. You may yearn for their occurrence, but you can't contrive anything. Don't make an attempt to work out prophecies. Believe and patience are the only enablers that actualize prophecy. Impatience dethrones kings. Every true kingdom is established by justice. It takes patience to get justice. God does not delay, but His timelines are not humanly designed. We have abandoned patience for faith alone. No normal person can stand with one leg for too long. We have a lot of teachings on faith, but few or none on patience.

That ye be not slothful, but followers of them who through faith and patience inherit the promises. {Hebrews 6:12 KJV}

Your promise of greatness can't be inherited until you master the process. The mastery can only be done if patience is made the vehicle. Shortcuts do not deliver lasting results. In fact, most shortcuts are found to turn into long cuts. Patience does not mean calmness necessarily, because the strong question is how do you identify a patient person? So, we shall begin to elucidate the steps that identify a patient individual.

Believe and patience are the only enablers that actualize prophecy.

## 1.	What do you look forward to: the result or the process?

Impatient people mistake gratification for result. One is instant, the other takes steps. Result lasts for a long time and can be replicated, but gratification comes in different shapes and forms. Do you prefer eating today and making tomorrow empty? Each time you put premium on the immediate profiteering of an exercise, you leave the future vacant. Genuine profits take time to mature. The bee does not make the beehive in a day.

Go ye therefore, and teach all nations, baptizing them in the name of the Father, and of the Son, and of the Holy Ghost: Teaching them to observe all things whatsoever I have commanded you: and, lo, I am with you always, even unto the end of the world. Amen. {**Matthew 28:19-20 KJV**}

The result is good, but it's only a small part of the game. Don't destroy the whole because of the negligible part.

(2)   **Time, an issue or not?**

Impatient people always have issues with time. It takes time to process an enviable future. True maturity comes with time. The hen can't hatch the eggs the day it lays them. Take time to brood on your dream. The fowl's eggs take about 21 days to be hatched. It sits on them to attain the required relative humidity. The hen demonstrates optimum patience the last 3 days before the chicks are hatched by not leaving the eggs at all. She sheds more weight during this process also. Simply because it knows its weight can destroy the eggs. How much weight have you lost for your future?

Whatsoever thy hand findeth to do, do it with thy might; for there is no work, nor device, nor knowledge, nor wisdom, in the grave, whither thou goest. {Ecc 9:10 KJV}

3.   Embrace mistakes

While mistakes must be avoided as much as possible, their presence brings improvement. You can't be better if you remain fixated on mistakes or its avoidance. Mistakes come through taking actions. If you don't act, you can't go wrong. Must you, therefore, make all the mistakes? Certainly, not. However, while it is better and safer to learn from the mistakes of others, you will not be immuned against them. Missing a step sometimes helps the individual to master the path better.

For a just man falleth seven times, and riseth up again: but the wicked shall fall into mischief. {Proverbs 24:16 KJV}

4.   Be kind to yourself

You must understand that things take time. No matter the art, relationships/results don't come with the swap of a hand. The people at the top today were at the bottom yesterday. Don't attempt to build your own Rome in a day. Reward and praise yourself for every little win. This act has a mental boost for the next challenge. Be less mindful of the amount of time it takes. Be more concerned with the progress made and the lesson learnt. Perhaps, the light bulb may not have seen the light-of-day, if Thomas Edison had been more preoccupied with the time spent.

And he saith unto them, Follow me, and I will make you fishers of men. And they straightway left their nets, and followed him. And going on from thence, he saw other two brethren, James the son of Zebedee, and John his brother, in a ship with Zebedee their father, mending their nets; and he called them. And they immediately left the ship and their father, and followed him. {**Matthew 4:19-22 KJV**}

Zebedee's sons hoped for a better future, so, they mended the net in anticipation. Can you imagine if their nets were not mended? When Christ Jesus arrived at the scene, they would have had none to let into the sea. They refused to be discouraged. Despite the disappointment through the night, they still mended their net. Nothing terminates progress like discouragement.

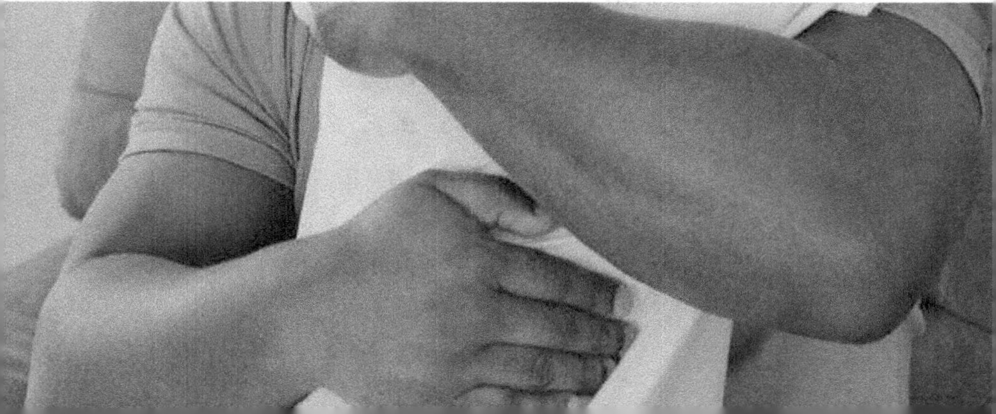
THE MINISTRY OF A FATHER,
OPTIONAL OR MANDATORY?

THE MINISTRY OF A FATHER: OPTIONAL OR MANDATORY?

And Elisha prayed, and said, LORD, I pray thee, open his eyes, that he may see. And the LORD opened the eyes of the young man; and he saw: and, behold, the mountain was full of horses and chariots of fire round about Elisha. And when they came down to him, Elisha prayed unto the LORD, and said, Smite this people, I pray thee, with blindness. And he smote them with blindness according to the word of Elisha. And Elisha said unto them, This is not the way, neither is this the city:

follow me, and I will bring you to the man whom ye seek. But he led them to Samaria. And it came to pass, when they were come into Samaria, that Elisha said, LORD, open the eyes of these men, that they may see. And the LORD opened their eyes, and they saw; and, behold, they were in the midst of Samaria. {II Kings 6:17-20 KJV}

You may afford to do without a father in all aspects but not direction and protection. In the anchor text above, the apprehension of the son was the intervention of a father. It takes the ministry of a father to point a faithful son to the protection and leverage God has provided. A time in ministry will come when your abode will be compassed by horses and chariots. You will require the word of a father. God obliged the prayer of Elisha in verse 17 of II Kings 6, because of the office he operated from. No doubt Elisha was a prolific prophet of God, but such emergency demand won't fail because of the principle of father-son dependence. One of the foremost responsibilities of a father is to provide security for the children and the entire family. This is God's direct delegated authority to fathers. The Almighty God protects His own. So, when a man operates in that office, he acts on His behalf. Could God not have protected the son of the prophet without necessarily allowing him to see the horses and the chariots? Yes! He could. However, the son of the prophet needed to be inducted into the ministry of fathers.

***Train up a child in the way he should go: and when he is old, he will not depart from it.* {Proverbs 22:6 KJV}**

In the day-to-day family realities, the male children are better taught parental responsibilities by observation. Whatever role(s) your children watch you discharge towards their mother and the family, they will replicate in the future. So, God was simply telling the servant of Elisha: *"This is how to be a father."* If kingship must be established you must optimize apprenticeship from a father. Even Saul could not captain Israel until a father sent him. Whose instruction(s) are you currently operating on? Saul could never have met Prophet Samuel without the instruction of Kish. Something bigger than the father's asses was a sake. There is a God factor in every father. If destiny struggles must be

averted, the instruction of a father must be taken seriously. You can't attain royalty without the assistance of a father. Your father is your root. The human race does not exist in a family tree for the fun of it.

And the asses of Kish Saul's father were lost. And Kish said to Saul his son, Take now one of the servants with thee, and arise, go seek the asses. [17] And when Samuel saw Saul, the LORD said unto him, Behold the man whom I spake to thee of! this same shall reign over my people. Then Saul drew near to Samuel in the gate, and said, Tell me, I pray thee, where the seer's house is. And Samuel answered Saul, and said, I am the seer: go up before me unto the high place; for ye shall eat with me today, and tomorrow I will let thee go, and will tell thee all that is in thine heart. And as for thine asses that were lost three days ago, set not thy mind on them; for they are found. And on whom is all the desire of Israel? Is it not on thee, and on all thy father's house? {**I Samuel 9:3, 17-20 KJV**}

Furthermore, a father exists for direction. Actually, the easiest way to initiate protection is through direction. Nations spend humongous amounts of their revenue on intelligence gathering because they know that safety is beyond kinetic approach alone. Losers are reactionary, winners are proactive. It takes information to be proactive. The father holds the key to some vital information in your life. No one can succeed as a son whose father has not graduated.

Saul was as successful as he was connected to Samuel. The throne eluded him the moment he began to treat Samuel's directives with levity. Arguably, Saul would have remained on the throne had he maintained alliance with Samuel. Nothing destroys royalty like disobedience to a father. Common sense would have shown Saul what Samuel represents. It took obedience to Samuel for Saul to discover the throne in I Samuel 10:1. Unfortunately, the disobedience of Saul in I Samuel 15 led to the loss of the throne. Don't rationalize the instruction of a father. God traditionally uses their voice to give direction. Though Eli didn't have a healthy relationship with God, yet God used his voice to call Samuel.

And the LORD called Samuel again the third time. And he arose and went to Eli, and said, Here am I; for thou didst call me. And Eli perceived that the LORD had called the child. Therefore Eli said unto Samuel, Go, lie down: and it shall be, if he call thee, that thou shalt say, Speak, LORD; for thy servant heareth. So Samuel went and lay down in his place. And the LORD came, and stood, and called as at other times, Samuel, Samuel. Then Samuel answered, Speak; for thy servant heareth. {I Samuel 3:8-10 KJV}

Every voice of God is preceded by the ministration of a son to a father. What service have you shown? Check I Samuel 3 verse 1 again! The call of Samuel was activated by his faithful service in the temple of Eli. The worst indiscipline in church today is the lack of guidance. Everyone wants to lead, no one wants to serve. A good leader must be a good follower. How do sons take orders from you when you are conspicuously disconnected from fathers?

And he saith unto them, Follow me, and I will make you fishers of men. And they straightway left their nets, and followed him. {Matthew 4:19-20 KJV}

The sons of Zebedee would have been poor, had they not plugged into the ministry of a father. Their father told them to mend their nets. Had they not mended their nets Christ Jesus would have come and passed them by. A lot of people miss out of divine arrangement because of this. There is always a precedent condition to every divine lifting. You won't quit if you listen to a father. One of his responsibilities is to tell you to stay on. No matter how things are bad today, keep mending your net. I imagine them abandoning their nets because of discouragement. So, despite a word from Christ, there won't have been a net. You may be going through shaking, mend the net. I am standing like Zebedee to tell you to mend your net for the great harvest ahead. Don't give up. You are about to get a net-breaking miracle. Just mend the net.

Have not I commanded thee? Be strong and of a good courage; be not afraid, neither be thou dismayed: for the LORD *thy God is with thee whithersoever thou goest.* {Joshua 1:9 KJV}

Never be too complacent or discouraged not to mend the net. The return on investment may currently be bad, invest again. The best time to sow is when the weather is not favourable. If you observe the weather, you might not sow.

Repetition is the surest pathway to mastery.

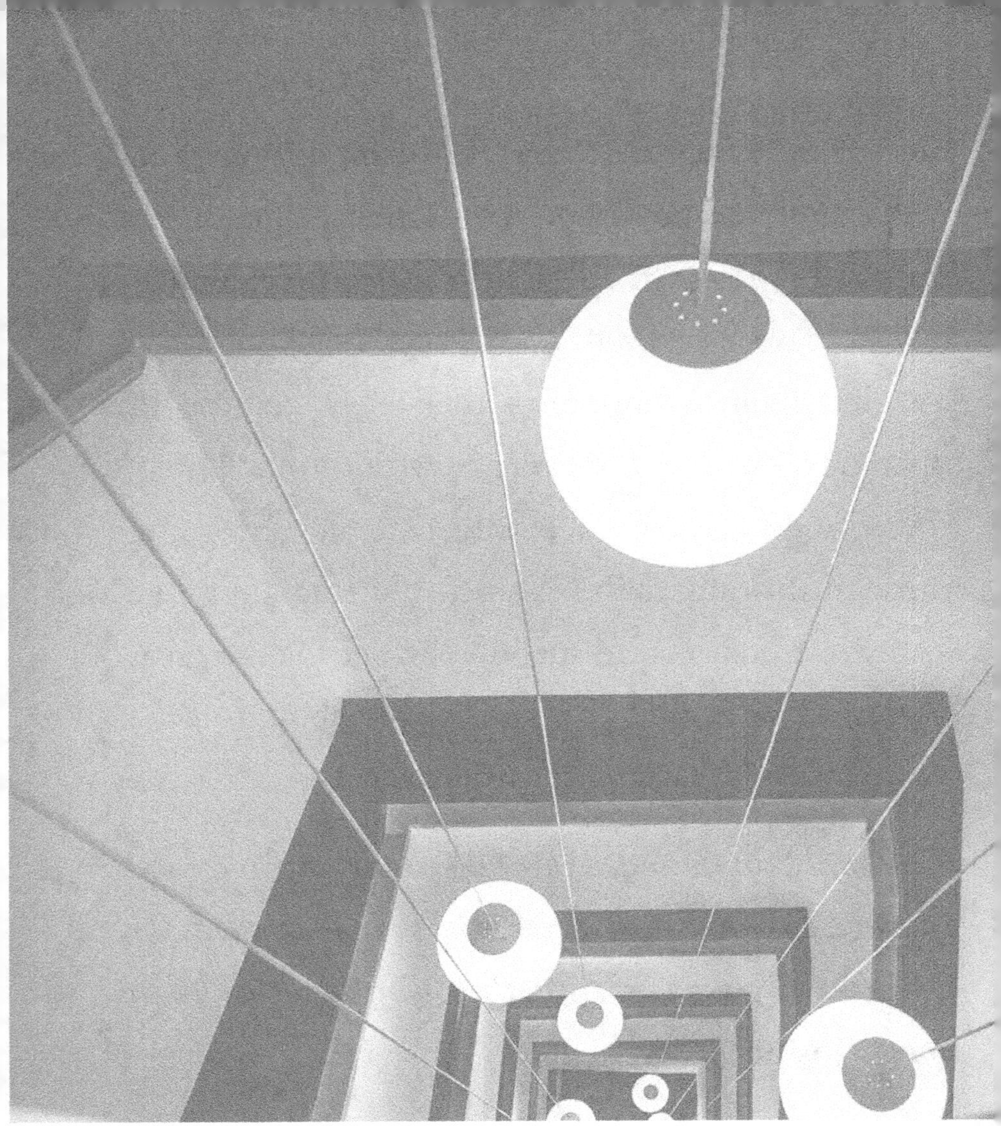

IS THERE NOT A CAUSE?

IS THERE NOT A CAUSE?

*A*nd David spake to the men that stood by him, saying, What shall be done to the man that killeth this Philistine, and taketh away the reproach from Israel? for who is this uncircumcised Philistine, that he should defy the armies of the living God? And the people answered him after this manner, saying, So shall it be done to the man that killeth him. And Eliab his eldest brother heard when he spake unto the men; and Eliab's anger was kindled against David, and he said, Why camest thou down hither? and with whom

hast thou left those few sheep in the wilderness? I know thy pride, and the naughtiness of thine heart; for thou art come down that thou mightest see the battle. And David said, What have I now done? Is there not a cause? And he turned from him toward another, and spake after the same manner: and the people answered him again after the former manner.
{I Samuel 17:26-30 KJV}

It takes a man who is destined for the throne to notice a vacuum in the palace. Nobility is not awarded, it is fought for. Challenges are roses hidden in thorns. Ladders present themselves as problems. No one dodges a fight that gets decorated. Until you see ahead, you can't see the throne. Ordinary men see human opposition, noble men see territorial resistance. You can't take the seat of any government except you first contend the lion and the bear. If you force yourself into the seat, exit becomes dishonourable. A crown is won. Beyond the resistance of Eliab were

> Nobility is not awarded it is fought for.

fundamental forces contending David's royalty. So, it was not Eliab who actually spoke, it was the powers dominating the territory. In verses 34 and 35, the statement of David clearly underscores the postulation above. He immediately shared the testimony of how he defeated the lion and the bear. What is a lion? The lion represents the head of a territory. So, the man mandated by the forces of the air to keep the area had handed over to David forcefully. Do you doubt that? Check verse 35. David addressed the lion as a "him" not "it". It was a deliberate choice of pronoun. While he used "it" for the sheep he kept, he chose to use "he/him" for the lion he killed. As soon as David secretly brought down the lion, the territory was effectively given to him. The crown you can't win in the secret can't be yours in the public. For every secret battle, there is an open reward.

But thou, when thou prayest, enter into thy closet, and when thou hast shut thy door, pray to thy Father which is in secret; and thy Father which seeth in secret shall reward thee openly. **{Matthew 6:6 KJV}**

Again, the teenager, David, announced the killing of a bear previously. That meant a lot to Saul and the elders of Israel who understood royalty. The bear speaks of the past. If you can't conquer your past you can't ascend to the throne. It

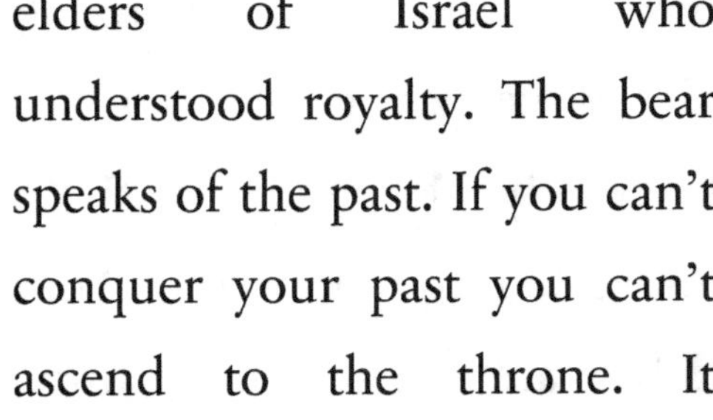

became obvious that David possessed the two most important pre-qualifications for the job. He was master of foundation and pattern. One's past is one's ancestral liabilities. You can't go far if you can't vacate them. The volunteer of David was not a careless one. He prepared for it. More importantly, he was anointed for it. It is one thing to possess the anointing, it's another thing to understand its essence. David knew why Prophet Samuel visited the house of Jesse on a fateful day.

And call Jesse to the sacrifice, and I will shew thee what thou shalt do: and thou shalt anoint unto me him whom I name unto thee. {1 Samuel 16:3KJV}

The steps and actions you take after a fellowship show whether there was an encounter or not. He resorted to the bush for a rehearsal. Men miss the offer of rising, because of lack of preparation. Chance comes to every man; the determinant of its utilization is preparation. According to Eliab, *"I have seen the nothingness of your heart."* To David, "there was a cause." If you paraphrase David's reply, it meant, *"I came because government is about to change hands."* Saul was hiding for 40 days, and Goliath came out to boast for the same number of days. The

So, the bigger the trouble, the mightier the trophy ahead.

one who can't command the troop can't be the commander-in-chief. The sound of the voice and the physique of Goliath alone intimidated Israel beyond measure. They could not phantom out the defeat of Goliath. Big problems usher in great announcements. So, the bigger the trouble the mightier the trophy ahead. They feared Goliath like a godless nation. Undoubtedly, Goliath was huge, about 9 feet tall. Goliath looked down on Israel until David showed up.

And it shall come to pass in that day, that the Lord shall set his hand again the second time to recover the remnant of his people, which shall be left, from Assyria, and from Egypt, and from Pathros, and from Cush, and from Elam, and from Shinar, and from Hamath, and from the islands of the sea. **{Isaiah 11:11 KJV}**

David wasn't seeing the height of Goliath, but the crown behind the victory. In Hebrews 12:2, scripture gave us a clear insight into why Christ Jesus was able to endure the pains and agonies of the cross. The glory behind the victory at the cross was His primary focus. If you can't picture the victory, you can't go through the shame of the process. Obstacles don't vacate the way; it takes a determined visionary man to remove them. Goliath doesn't stop willingly; they are stopped by people with a will. God heard Goliath's boastings. He demanded for a man from Israel; God sent a teenager to humiliate him. No matter the circumstance, don't threaten God's people. Don't threaten anyone who hides under the name of God. When men fail and boys are available, the boys become men.

Saying, Touch not mine anointed, and do my prophets no harm. {**Ps. 105: 15**

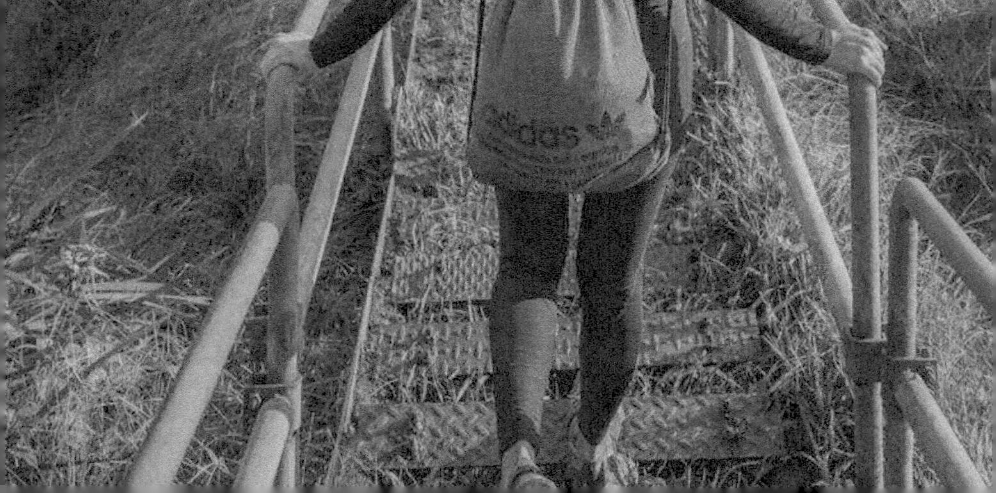

TAKING MORE STEPS

I press toward the mark for the prize of the high calling of God in Christ Jesus. {Philippians 3:14 KJV}

The most potent strategy for bringing Goliath down is the ability to take another step. As unsavoury as failure might be, a life of mediocrity is worse. A mediocre is someone who started well but stopped halfway. The likes of Eliab and Saul began well but allowed the intimidation of Goliath to stop them. How does a whole troop stop in one spot for 40 days? They became highly indecisive. The unrelenting advancement of David towards Goliath {I Samuel 17: 48) gave him the victory. God does not ever want His people to stop. In Exodus 14:13, Moses applied Israel's strategy of waiting and bemoaning the situation. In verse 15, God sharply disagreed with Moses. ***"… and the Lord said unto Moses, wherefore criest thou unto me? Speak unto the children of Israel, that they go forward…"*** God never condones crying; it is a sign of defeat. Whatever the battle before you now, face it squarely your God is with you. Don't cry. Apart from being broken in His presence in worship, the believer is not permitted to cry.

And all wept, and bewailed her: but he said, Weep not; she is not dead, but sleepeth. And they laughed him to scorn, knowing that she was dead. {Luke 8:52-53 KJV}

If you stop at the killing of the lion and bear alone, you can't get to the palace. Whatever achievement recorded so far, should be seen as a stepping stone.

The throne is the next glory. The challenge is the inability to follow through. No greatness is attained at the first attempt. It will make no news if you announce the death of the lion and the bear. Everyone possesses a fantastic curriculum vitae. The differentiation is excelling beyond set records. Begin by working for free. David killed the lion and bear without payment. The lion and bear you kill when nobody is there determines the Goliath you will kill when everyone is there. David negotiated when the bigger stage came. What shall be done for the man? David enquired gently. He knew that Goliath was already a prey. David took five unique steps that made him outstanding. We shall consider the steps.

For God is not unrighteous to forget your work and labour of love, which ye have shewed toward his name, in that ye have ministered to the saints, and do minister. And we desire that every one of you do shew the same diligence to the full assurance of hope unto the end: {Hebrews 6:10-11 KJV}

1.   Continuous improvement

Any anointing that does not drive you into a continuous improvement is a waste. The proof of David's anointing was constant visibility. As soon as Prophet Samuel anointed David, he never slid into obscurity. The first step the anointed must take is the move of service. If David was not given to service, he may not have killed Goliath. He didn't come to the field primarily for Goliath, but to serve the brothers. The brothers were trained soldiers. The sign that you are called to the palace is to master the honour of kings. Royalty is learnt. If your life is not given to restrictions, you may fail even as a king. Kings don't talk anyhow.

Neither, because they are the seed of Abraham, are they all children: but, In Isaac shall thy seed be called. **{Romans 9:7 KJV}**

What have you stopped, because of where you are going to? If your dream is not big enough to sacrifice for, why should God enable it? What skills have you learnt because of the future ahead of you? Your belief in your tomorrow is evident in the steps you take today.

2.   Discover you and what works for you

But be ye doers of the word, and not hearers only, deceiving your own selves. For if any be a hearer of the word, and not a doer, he is like unto a man beholding his natural face in a glass: For he beholdeth himself, and goeth his way, and straightway forgetteth what manner of man he was. But whoso looketh into the perfect law of liberty, and continueth therein, he being not a forgetful hearer, but a doer of the work, this man shall be blessed in his deed. {James 1:22-25 KJV}

Again, David understood the importance and potency of the strings/stone at that time. What you follow determines what follows you. Self-awareness

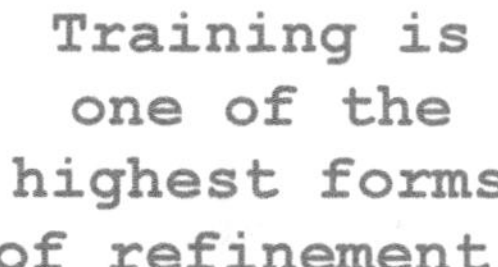

is an indispensable route to greatness. How much of yourself do you understand? David knew that the armour of Saul would limit him. Do you know what limits you? Your strength is in your uniqueness. Imitation of others is abandonment of your dream. Don't step out of your track. We're created and designed in line with purposes we are sent to fulfill. You are not inferior to anyone, neither is your vision. There is no calling without glory. The icing of a cake makes the difference. Develop yourself in line with your calling. It takes a refined man to travel far. Training is one of the highest forms of refinement.

3.   Focus

I will set no wicked thing before mine eyes: I hate the work of them that turn aside; it shall not cleave to me. {PS. 101:3 KJV}

Let thine eyes look right on, and let thine eyelids look straight before thee. {Proverbs 4: 25 KJV}

Whatever you give constant attention to, you master. Be a master of one aspect. You should have primary goals you put your attention on. Where are you now? And where is the next level? If you must be an achiever, you must face a task at a time. Once one's attention is divided, failure becomes the next outcome. The surest sign of growth and development is focus. Projects succeed or fail depending on the level of attention we assign to them. Everyone can be productive if only they can focus. You must set your priorities right. What matters to you must be tailored to your goals. Forget the objectiv1es of the process they embarked on. Focus helps you to organize yourself. Extraordinary great men like Samson were brought to their knees for loss of focus. The atmosphere you permit around you depends on your priorities. Those who are faced with serious goals don't have time for frivolities.

As soon as David took his attention from the enemy, the wife of Uriah got his attention (II Samuel 11:5-27). The easiest and surest way to refuse sin is to be focused on an assignment. Idleness is the tangible reality of loss of focus.

4.   Self -Discipline

For in many things we offend all. If any man offend not in word, the same is a perfect man, and able also to bridle the whole body. {James 3:2 KJV}

The strongest army one can conquer is self. If you can tame your tendencies, you can govern the world. You must understand yourself, to control same. What are your weaknesses? There are actually no strong men, but disciplined men. The ability to understand the things that trigger your weaknesses is the beginning of strength. In Proverbs 4:23, you are admonished to guard the heart

(mind). This is the center of activities. Whatever can't get to your mind can't conquer you. You are what you think the most. Utterances are produced out of the abundance of the mind. Never allow your mouth to say everything that goes through your mind. Learn to moderate your thoughts.

A good man out of the good treasure of his heart bringeth forth that which is good; and an evil man out of the evil treasure of his heart bringeth forth that which is evil: for of the abundance of the heart his mouth speaketh. {Luke 6:45 KJV}

Self-discipline is the rare ability to lead oneself aright. If you can't guide yourself properly, leading others will be disastrous. It is said that charity begins from home. Sign off from greatness if self-discipline is a complex subject for you.

5. Giving/forgiving

Be not deceived; God is not mocked: for whatsoever a man soweth, that shall he also reap. {Galatians 6:7 KJV}

Judge not, and ye shall not be judged: condemn not, and ye shall not be condemned: forgive, and ye shall be forgiven: **Luke 6:37 KJV}**

Unforgiveness can be cartooned as a man attempting to move forward while looking backward. No doubt, the individual will have a great fall. Good givers are good forgivers. David could focus on the battle with Goliath because he forgave his brothers for the harassment. Also, he was in the battlefield to care for them. Your distractors don't deserve your attention. Why devote a portion of your heart to your mockers? Only results silence troublemakers. Eliab faded away as soon as David killed Goliath. The more wins you pursue, the less relevant your opposers become. The only way they can't pull you down is to go higher. The greatest concern of your enemy is your victory and happiness.

THE ENEMY TO FLEE FROM

Flee fornication. Every sin that a man doeth is without the body; but he that committeth fornication sinneth against his own body. {I Corinthians 6:18 KJV}

We have reviewed and analyzed various impediments likely to stop a king. Interestingly, whether already discussed or not, all can be combated except one. We have often alluded to the fact that David fought 66 battles and triumphed in all. That remains true. However, the fact is, David faltered in one battle. We seem to sideline the contest over Uriah's wife. King David was gallant both for the enemies within his household and outside. He undermined the instruction of I Corinthians 6:18. Defeating the lion, the king of the jungle, was not a mere feat to accomplish. But he did overcome the lion and went ahead to defeat the bear. He was relegated to his knees by the wife of Uriah. The only existing strategy to overcome the wife of Uriah would have been to flee.

And it came to pass in an eveningtide, that David arose from off his bed, and walked upon the roof of the king's house: and from the roof he saw a woman washing herself; and the woman was very beautiful to look upon. **{II Samuel 11:2 KJV}**

Joseph attained the throne unblemished. Probably, he may have done a personal study of the things that destroy greatness. He perhaps came to the conclusion that he can handle all except Potiphar's wife. He combated the pit and overcame the Ishmaelites but fled from Potiphar's wife. Though Joseph could not boast of killing neither a lion nor a bear, but he emerged successful. If you preview the life and times of David and Joseph, Joseph may become more outstanding. He left no dirt on his pilgrimage from his father's house to the seat of a prime minister. What a laudable successful career he enjoyed. He knew that to be unjustly incarcerated is a less mental torture. He didn't want to enjoy temporal lifting. Joseph got the opportunity to enjoy the sin and cover it up with a lie. He was fully aware that a little lie would put the crown in the hand of the devil. When men lie, men hand over their thrones to Satan. That is exactly what a lie does.

Ye are of your father the devil, and the lusts of your father ye will do. He was a murderer from the beginning, and abode not in the truth, because there is no truth in him. When he speaketh a lie, he speaketh of his own: for he is a liar, and the father of it. {John 8:44 KJV}

It is not a coincidence that Samson equally killed a lion, but suffered in the hands of Delilah. How do you reconcile a battle expert like Samson falling cheaply for Delilah? The only escape route before Samson was to flee. Making explanations and riddles in the face of a ballistic missile is monumental foolishness of the first order. Even Christ Jesus said, "*…go and sin no more…*" The "*go*" preceded the "*sin no more*". This implies you must flee before you rationalize the next step of action. You don't contemplate in the face of a fatal accident you can't recover from.

When Jesus had lifted up himself, and saw none but the woman, he said unto her, Woman, where are those thine accusers? hath no man condemned thee? She said, No man, Lord. And Jesus said unto her, Neither do I condemn thee: go, and sin no more. {John 8:10-11 KJV}

If you must arrive safely at your destination for the coronation you must "*go*". To "*go*" is synonymous to "*flee*." In Proverbs 6:27, what Solomon expressed is in the form of a rhetorical question. "*Can a man take fire in his bosom and his clothes not be burned?*" No matter the level of intelligence and information gathering at your disposal, a Delilah will menace you up. Because

Samson thought he could play around the emotions of Delilah and escape. As a warrior of repute, he had significant intelligence about the antics and tactics of the Philistines.

No matter what you already know about Delilah and Potiphar's wife, the only door of escape is to flee. You can't discuss and deliberate with Delilah and not be destroyed. We shall be studying the fleeing strategies available to everyone who must taste greatness.

Neither give place to the devil. **{Ephesians 4:27 KJV}**

(1)   Make it inconvenient

If you allow immoral advances to be attractive, you will fall for them. Make your communication plain without unnecessary encumbrances. If the atmosphere permits it, you have allowed it already. It might sometimes begin with immoral and unholy suggestions. Arguably, Joseph had the opportunity to escape going to prison. He stayed within the radius and magnetic field of sin for long. It was not the first day Potiphar's wife made advances that she forced him. Why did Joseph believe he could handle the master's wife? A well-defined no, perhaps, a public no would have been offered. Once you perceive the smell of a poisonous gas you flee. You don't wait to confirm if it is what you think. Immorality alienates one from God. Be quick to declare your stand. Don't wait for all sins to be presented as a menu before you speak up. Whatever you don't see or hear your mind can't dwell on. Close up your input devices, so, your spirit is safeguarded.

***Not that which goeth into the mouth defileth a man; but that which cometh out of the mouth, this defileth a man.* {Matthew 15:11 KJV}**

2.   Agree it is Destructive

Your refusal of an immoral life is never a favour to God. Some handle sin as though they're doing someone good by remaining holy. Uprightness only makes the believer go upward. God will remain God irrespective of how you live your life. Nothing can diminish the Almightiness of God. He will remain supreme. It's the believer's life that dwindles depending on his habits. Never permit any habit that makes you unstable. Refuse any shadow of double-mindedness. Can you look up and view down simultaneously? Submission to God means total agreement with His word. A righteous man is one who places the most premium on His instruction.

For this is the will of God, even your sanctification, that ye should abstain from fornication: {I Thess. 4:3 KJV}

3.   Think of the consequences

Actions and choices attract consequences. Whatever move you make now will either make or mar you. Nothing is ever a secret. Even if hell does not exist, the consequence of sin still makes it unattractive. The earthly repercussion of indulgence in ungodly acts is disastrous, and stifles your boldness before the throne. Sin takes the believer away from the location God kept him/her. Adam could not be seen, because of a wrong choice. If God can't locate you, He can't bless you. Your blessing is in your location. You can only grow where He has planted you. This is the justification of why people do well in careers where others are frustrated.

Let us break their bands asunder, and cast away their cords from us. **{Psalm 1:3 KJV}**

4.   Prayers

The surest way to remain standing is by prayers. The assumption that you can't fall is too expensive to be taken far. Nothing strengthens humanity like prayers. Every man at his best is nothing without God.

Prayers mingle humanity with divinity. Your progression rate is your depth in prayers. Pray in words and in kind. Your actions and inactions are prayers. So, be circumspect in what you do. The closer you move to God, the less flesh can control you. A man of the Spirit is led of God. Don't take any step except you pray first. Prayer is the process of deadness to the world. Except you live above them, you can't reign above them. Whatever controls you is your master.

*Neither yield ye your members as instruments of unrighteousness unto sin: but yield yourselves unto God, as those that are alive from the dead, and your members as instruments of righteousness unto God. For sin shall not have dominion over you: for ye are not under the law, but under grace. {**Romans 6:13-14 KJV**}*

COMMUNION BUILDS INTIMACY

COMMUNION BUILDS INTIMACY

Henceforth I call you not servants; for the servant knoweth not what his lord doeth: but I have called you friends; for all things that I have heard of my Father I have made known unto you. {John 15:15 KJV}

That I may know him, and the power of his resurrection, and the fellowship of his sufferings, being made conformable unto his death; {Philli. 3:10 KJV}

No one can enjoy kingship that is disconnected from the paramount ruler. You can't be empowered in a kingdom you are not known. Before you make any choice, ask God to guide you. The higher His guidance the closer your proximity to Him. The understanding of people is superficial from a distance. Until you are close to Him you are not known. You can't be a person of the God you hardly fellowship with. Let God be your moderator. Everything appears good on the surface until analysed. For instance, it is not every woman you marry. She can be born again and still not be for Him. God's inspiration should drive your aspirations. Even Christ Jesus

withdrew Himself from people. He used to stay apart to fellowship. The pathway of renewal is by the fellowship with the Spirit. He didn't commit Himself to any man. Not everyone in a celebration ceremony is present to rejoice with the celebrant. Be careful how you lose your guard. Be sensitive is the minimum requirement in a wicked world.

If there be therefore any consolation in Christ, if any comfort of love, if any fellowship of the Spirit, if any bowels and mercies, {Phili 2:1 KJV}

The more of fellowship you enjoy the less of others you see. If you are still preoccupied with the errors of others, you lack intimacy with Him. In this Christian race, nobody is a referee. It takes a sinner to identify a sinner. If your focus is on pleasing the Master, you can hardly notice who is going wrong. Idleness triggers envy. When you see people always have time for others, check what their businesses are. Don't be excited with negative news of others. The closer to God you go the more love you demonstrate towards humanity. Stop the pull-him-down syndrome. The more you invest efforts in raising others, the higher you go. So, help people without strings attached. Graduate from being a clergy to being a father to your members as a pastor. You enjoy yourself better when you are committed to the growth of others. Even if you have no physical substance to offer, give hope. How do you feel when people leave a local assembly because of your actions or inaction? Be an encouragement to people, not discouragement.

And let us consider one another to provoke unto love and to good works: Not forsaking the assembling of ourselves together, as the manner of some is; but exhorting one another: and so much the more, as ye see the day approaching. {**Hebrews 10:24-25 KJV**}

You can't pull down anyone you didn't lift. It takes less energy to help than to pull down. If you fellowship with the Holy Spirit, the love for others will overwhelm you. Make up your mind so there will not be jealousy or hate in your mind. Leave people with lasting memories of you. Bad people leave their victims with lessons. Good people leave happiness behind for every encounter you have with them. Do you know the best encounter? It comes from the best kind of people, sweet memories. Do people miss you when you leave, or do they thank

God that you left? People are not afraid of you; it is your foolishness they avoid.

(1)   Submission to authority

Remember them which have the rule over you, who have spoken unto you the word of God: whose faith follow, considering the end of their conversation. **{Hebrews 13:7KJV}.**

One of the ways to initiate and sustain communion with God is through submission to headship. Your obedience to lawful instructions speaks volumes about your fellowship with the Holy Spirit. Carnal people are difficult to control or lead. They attach fleshly interpretations and meanings to every move. The things of the Spirit are not most times logical. Every authority, especially in the house of God is constituted by Him. God established leadership for order and direction (Romans 13:1). The more you are lost in Him, the deeper humility you demonstrate towards man. A proud person can't be a spiritual person. One of the first steps of intimacy with God is bridleness of the tongue. There are unguarded statements you should not make about those God has placed over you. If you can tame your tongue, your life can be directed. Acceleration in life and destiny is a product of direction.

2.   Forgive them

Then said Jesus, Father, forgive them; for they know not what they do. And they parted his raiment, and cast lots. {Luke 23:34 KJV}.

A spiritual man is one who understands the mystery of forgiveness. Vengeance is a sure tool of the believer's advancement. However, a call for it can't be executed by the celestials except you let the individual go off your mind. No one is big enough to be imprisoned in your mind. God can't fight your battles except you forgive the individual. Also, forgiveness helps you to

A spiritual man is one who understands the mystery of forgiveness.

maintain a steady flow with the Holy Spirit. He can't fellowship with a vessel that is not free and empty. The walk with the Holy Spirit is hinged on grace and mercy. You can't enjoy mercy except you normalize showing others mercy. Separate the person from the wrong habits.

With the merciful thou wilt shew thyself merciful; with an upright man thou wilt shew thyself upright; {Ps. 18:25 KJV}.

3.   Study the scriptures

The first step you must learn in discipleship is discipline. You can't walk with God except you are amenable to learning. You can't know God except you read God. Even Christ Jesus read the scriptures in the temple. It was customary of Him to do so {Luke 4:17-21). His assignment was written in the scriptures. Yours can't be different. The more of God you discover, the more of self is revealed. You can't possess what you lack revelation of. If you don't know the letters, how can you get the Spirit behind the letters? The scripture is God's written prayer point to man. So, the words caught His attention more than anything.

Who also hath made us able ministers of the new testament; not of the letter, but of the spirit: for the letter killeth, but the spirit giveth life. {II Cor. 3:6 KJV}.

Studying scriptures is not optional. There is equally no alternative to it. It is a discipline you must imbibe. This is the minimum subscription you must maintain in this kingdom to keep receiving signals. God does not speak outside of His revealed word. The highest encounter is revelation. Nothing exists except they are first revealed. The knowledge of the word helps you to argue your case. Prayer is like a lawyer standing before a judge for pleadings. The judge can't grant the pleadings not brought before him. You either win or lose your case depending on the depth of your jurisprudence. The Bible is your daily law report. It is renewed on a daily basis. You can't afford to use stale knowledge of law to argue current cases in court.

Come now, and let us reason together, saith the LORD: though your sins be as scarlet, they shall be as white as snow; though they be red like crimson, they shall be as wool. {Isaiah 1:18 KJV}.

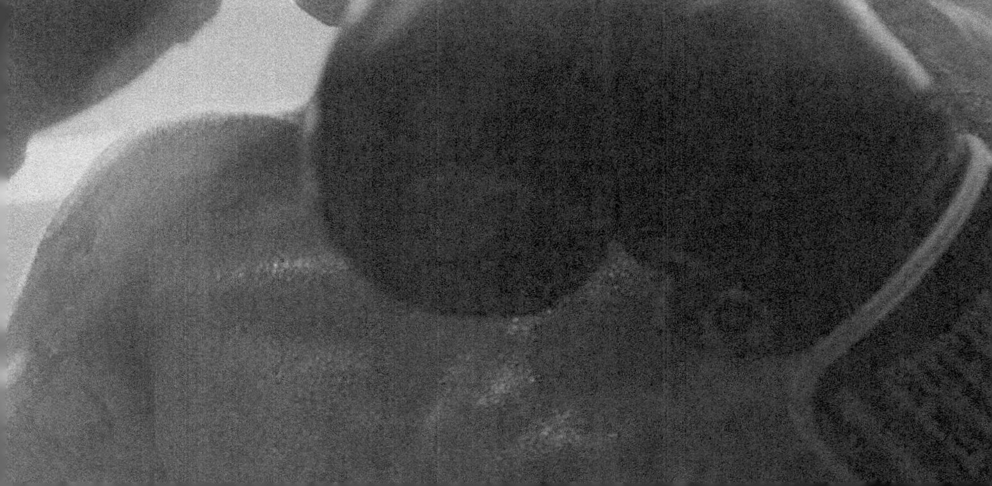
WHEN A MAN FIGHTS SELF

WHEN A MAN FIGHTS SELF

*A**nd Moab shall be destroyed from being a people, because he hath magnified himself against the* LORD. *{Jeremiah 48:42KJV}*

The most difficult diagnosis is when there is a systemic organ failure. When a system in danger spreads to other organs thereby incapacitating them. Sepsis can be life-threatening. Now, people trigger failure in their lives and terminate their own ascension to relevance. In the opening text of this chapter, Moab was going to be wiped out from the earth. Why will this extreme punishment be meted on a people? The latter part of the same verse answered the question almost immediately. Can you imagine a mortal man or people fighting God? The fastest way to fall into an endless ditch in life is to be appositive to God. How do people willfully stand against what God stands for? In agreement with the songwriter, *"no one can battle with the Lord."* In Isaiah 13:19, God compared the destruction of Babylon with the obliteration of Sodom and Gomorrah. A world power at some point became ruined because they aligned against the interest of God. We shall study how nations or individuals destroyed themselves. When external forces or enemies are contending with your rising, it is easier to stop than when you are against yourself. People hardly admit that they are behind their own woes.

I.   Pride

But he giveth more grace. Wherefore he saith, God resisteth the proud, but giveth grace unto the humble. **{James 4:6 KJV}**

God is the enemy of a proud man or nation. You can either invite God to fight you or lift you depending on the attitude you display. People fall from grace when they can't see errors or take corrections. Pride

When no one can call you to order, you are set for self-destruction.

is the purveyor of shame and resistance. When God resists you, men disdain you. A proud man is one who views himself higher than where he has been placed. When no one can call you to order, you are set for self-destruction. Who do you revere? It is foolishness when you hear people say, *"They fear no man."* There must be someone who can call you to order. Stop acting with impunity. Being simple is a manifestation of humility. The more complex your things are the more you set yourself against God. Imagine God blocking assistance from getting to you.

The fear of the LORD is to hate evil: pride, and arrogancy, and the evil way, and the froward mouth, do I hate. {Proverbs 8:13 KJV}

Avoid being complicated. Life is simple. An arrogant person sees everyone wrong except himself. He delightfully talks down on people without any remorse. The arrogant sees himself as untouchable. They correct others but see correction as opposition. Be open to learning. It can come from anyone, whether higher or lower. In Romans 12:16, the scripture urges us to condescend to men of low estate. Be quick to reach out to people lower than your social class. When you make access to you impossible, you make learning difficult. You have a lot to learn from the downtrodden. A proud man amplifies himself.

But he that glorieth, let him glory in the Lord. For not he that commendeth himself is approved, but whom the Lord commendeth. {II Cor. 10:17-18 KJV}

Humility brings honor. Do you want to be lifted or promoted, humble yourself. Serve both your seniors and juniors in the office. Be less concerned about the haughty who will take advantage of your simplicity. Definitely, some will. Don't mind the attitude of people. Don't let it stop you from doing the needful.

Whatever you confirm to be the right attitude should be practiced.

ii.   Penchant for self-centeredness

(For many walk, of whom I have told you often, and now tell you even weeping, that they are the enemies of the cross of Christ: Whose end is destruction, whose God is their belly, and whose glory is in their shame, who mind earthly things.) **{Philippians 3:18-19 KJV}**

According to Apostle Paul, he wept while addressing this vice in the above verses. People make themselves enemies of the cross when gains at the expense of others is their drive. They will stop at nothing to make merchandise of the gospel. Several individuals nowadays commercialize the gifts and callings of God. There is nothing wrong when people bless you with their carnal things. But a lot is amiss when you take advantage of people. Some even dubiously resort to gimmicks just to make gains. Your primary focus should not be about self. When you are genuinely committed to the gospel, God will lift you beyond your dreams. There must be a difference between the people of the world and the kingdom-oriented ones. Proverbs 21:31 should restrain you from taking to self-help. No matter the economic uncertainty out there, God should be your primary supplier. Whatever labour you exert outside of God leads to futility. Ultimately, according to John 3:27, "... *no man can receive anything except it is given from above...*" You set your life for destruction by being an enemy of the cross of Christ.

Except the LORD build the house, they labour in vain that build it: except the LORD keep the city, the watchman waketh but in vain. {Ps. 127:1 KJV}

God is more concerned about your motives than your actions. Preaching the gospel is commanded, nevertheless, what is your motive of doing it? Do you call for giving to enrich yourself or to open channels of blessing for the people?

You must be a self-moderator and regulator of the steps you take. Your motivation is key. Learn to self-examine yourself. Otherwise, you program your life for a fall by your actions.

Let your loins be girded about, and your lights burning; {Luke 12:35 KJV}

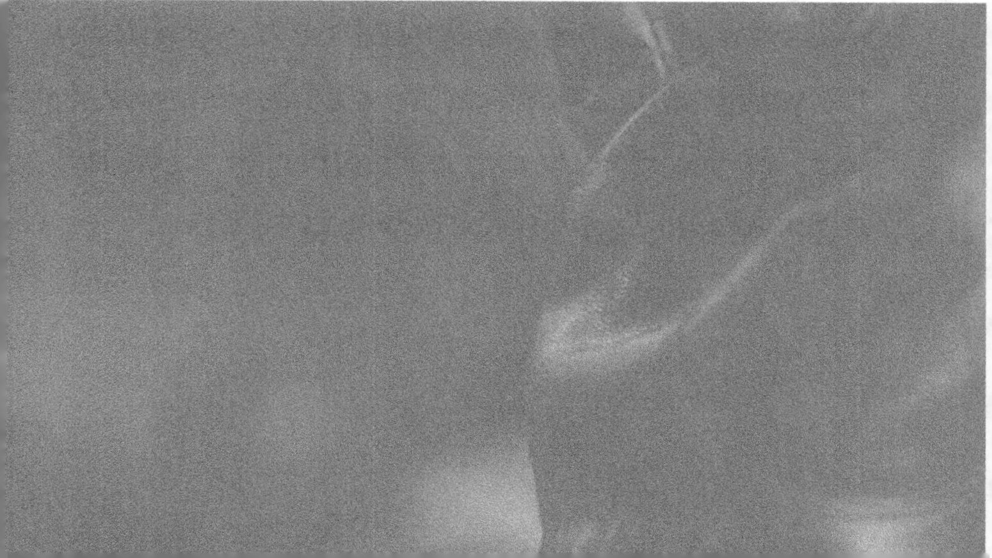

OBSERVE THE HIDDEN TIME

OBSERVE THE HIDDEN TIME

nd when they were departed, behold, the angel of the Lord appeareth to Joseph in a dream, saying, Arise, and take the young child and his mother, and flee into Egypt, and be thou there until I bring thee word: for Herod will seek the young child to destroy him. When he arose, he took the young child and his mother by night, and departed into Egypt: {Matthew 2:13-14 KJV}

Countless kings have been stopped from ascending the throne because they prematurely showed themselves. Mary, the earthly mother of Christ Jesus, could have been vociferous about the birth of the child and destroyed the baby. Every greatness is nurtured in the secret. Don't announce yourself before the Herods of this world when the time is not ripe. There are set times for everything in life.

The Herods who destroy infant kings are still in our cities, towns, and villages. Be careful who and when you share your testimony. If you step out earlier than your time, God won't protect you. Could not God have killed the Herod who sought the life of Christ Jesus? Remember, Herod eventually paid the supreme price. The timing is an important component in God's divine agenda. He does not go outside of the timing. Everything in this world has been programmed already. Be sensitive to work within the stipulated time. In your hidden time and place, there are lessons you must learn.

And the woman conceived, and bare a son: and when she saw him that he was a goodly child, she hid him three months. {Exodus 2:2 KJV}'

The wisdom of Moses' mother saved the Israelites from the land of the Egyptians. According to Exodus 2:2, she hid the child as soon as she noticed he was a goodly one. Firstly, she was sensitive to discern the future of the child. She saw a messiah than a mere child. It is one thing to understand, it is a different thing to take the right step. Hiding the child was another divine intelligence she demonstrated. Prior to this time, scripture didn't record that any of the Jewish women did what she did. They sheepishly never saw a single star in the male infants nor made attempts to preserve their lives. People submit to the whims and caprices of the destroyers when they are spiritually blind. It took Moses' mother to remotely see the emancipation of Israel ahead of time. How else can you sum up her actions? The goodliest thing about Moses was the freedom of Israel and the birth of a new nation. She took the life of the baby in her own hands. And God backed her up. There is always a place for common sense in destiny's progression.

The lips of the righteous feed many: but fools die for want of wisdom. **{Proverbs 10:21 KJV}**

Again, she patiently played along with the daughter of Pharaoh. Wisdom restrained her from being loquacious about the actual identity of Moses. Had Moses been borne by some women today, the folly of the mother would have terminated his dream prematurely. This is the generation where mothers post their minute-old babies on social media platforms. More than enthusiasm, it is lack of spiritual depth. Even the medical profession recognizes that infants have little or no immunity to ward off diseases and therefore should be shielded. Can't you learn spiritual things from medical sense? Why kill the innocent baby because you want to project over bloated image of yourself? Stop this nonsense and adopt the mind of God.

Let this mind be in you, which was also in Christ Jesus: {**Phili2:5 KJV**}

Was Christ Jesus to be here again today as an infant, God will still instruct Joseph to escape with the child to Egypt. Don't be wiser than scriptures. Stop announcing your dreams. Don't announce your foundation, let the roof announce it. Stop spiritualizing your being a talkative. The devil can't stop you from actualizing your destiny if you learn to succeed privately.

Be mature and sophisticated for the devil to handle cheaply.

Some national prophecies have been fought because they were made public instead of an *intel* for the church. I stopped announcing most national prophetic intelligence, except God specifically instructs otherwise. Be mature and sophisticated for the devil to handle cheaply.

And when they were departed, behold, the angel of the Lord appeareth to Joseph in a dream, saying,

Arise, and take the young child and his mother, and flee into Egypt, and be thou there until I bring thee word: for Herod will seek the young child to destroy him. When he arose, he took the young child and his mother by night, and departed into Egypt: {**Matthew 2:13-14 KJV**}

Have you noticed that David used the same strategy to come to limelight? He went underground as soon as Samuel anointed him. Until he successfully killed the lion and the bear, he never showed up. Obtain a testimony before you proclaim yourself. Don't announce your appointment letter; let the official uniform publicize you. It takes common sense to be wise. Saul would never have led Israel had he told the uncle what Prophet Samuel told him.

And Saul said unto his uncle, He told us plainly that the asses were found. But of the matter of the kingdom, whereof Samuel spake, he told him not. {**I Samuel 10:16 KJV**}

Have you passed the exams life set before you? Countless spinsters have had their relationships broken, because of premature announcement of same. Scriptures advise us to love everyone. Love is never synonymous to trust. You are safer when you trust none or few. The devil uses your close allies to perpetuate wickedness most times. Check the people who cause the most devastating pains, they're usually close people. Don't entrust information to people you have not tried. Trust must come from long time test, if at all it should, be aware of this. It is not everyone who comes around you who is a helper. People can do anything just to get your favour. The Lord brings helpers around you, as much as the devil brings destroyers.

The thief cometh not, but for to steal, and to kill, and to destroy: I am come that they might have life, and that they might have it more abundantly. **{John 10:10 KJV}**

The success or otherwise of the devil depends largely on you. You must be sensitive to detect him. Avoid sentiments. Disloyal people anywhere are disloyal people everywhere. Don't bring anyone close if he/she has a previous history of disloyalty to the former boss. We are often blind to people's tendencies because of foolish hope that they will change. People consolidate their characters, they hardly change. Don't offer your life as a specimen. You might not be fortunate to recover from it. Mark early signs of disloyalty and negative traits. However, some mistakes can be corrected over time through training. But, a disloyal and unteachable individual should not be accommodated.

Poverty and shame shall be to him that refuseth instruction: but he that regardeth reproof shall be honoured. {**Proverbs 13:18 KJV**}

Unteachable people don't observe protocols. You can't survive around greatness except you master the observation of protocols. There are languages you must never use in the presence or absence of your helper. Those who do not honour your boss can't be your allies. How much of time do they respect? Any man or woman who has little or no respect for your time will eventually destroy you. Your highest value is your time. These are the habits infant kings learn in the early days when they are hidden. The hiding process or days are for lessons. How much you learn will determine how swift you rise to the throne. Be swift, but even more so be impactful.

Rest in the LORD, and wait patiently for him: fret not thyself because of him who prospereth in his way, because of the man who bringeth wicked devices to pass. {Ps37:7 KJV}

Don't rush your process. Embrace it.